This book is dedicated to everyone who has ever laughed at their own trumps!

Also, special thanks to my sister, Lynn, for the hours spent co-editing, travelling by train between London and Liverpool.

And thanks to Kate for all the finishing touches.

Library of Congress Cataloging-in-Publication Data

Roberts, David, 1970-
Pee-ew! Is that you, Bertie? / David Roberts.
p. cm.
Summary: Bertie's family complains when he farts at the dentist's office, the museum, in the café, and in the playhouse, but he knows that they can be equally as stinky even though they try to hide their farts.
ISBN 0-8109-5014-6
[1. Flatulence—Fiction. 2. Behavior—Fiction.] I. Title.

PZ7.R5415Pe 2004
[E]—dc22
2004005387

First published in Great Britain by Little Tiger Press
Copyright © David Roberts

Published in 2004 by Harry N. Abrams, Incorporated, New York.
All rights reserved. No part of the contents of this book may be reproduced without the written permission of the publisher.

Printed and bound in Belgium
10 9 8 7 6 5 4 3 2

Harry N. Abrams, Inc.
100 Fifth Avenue
New York, NY 10011
www.abramsbooks.com

Abrams is a subsidiary of

PEE-EW!
Is That You, Bertie?

David Roberts

Harry N. Abrams, Inc., Publishers

This is Bertie.
He likes making smells.

PFOOF

Bertie farted at the dentist.
It was smelly!

"PEE-EW! Is that You, Bertie?

That's not good manners," sniffed Mom.

PARP

Bertie let off a bigger one in the museum and giggled. No one else did. It stank.

"PEE-EW!
Is that You, Bertie?

I've never been so embarrassed," sniffed Dad.

At the café Bertie let off a really regal one.
It smelled worse than a rotten egg.

"PEE-EW! Is that You, Bertie?"

It's not nice to pass gas in the café—not when people are eating," sniffed Grandma.

Bertie let rip a big one in his sister Suzy's playhouse. It reeked. Suzy was livid.

"PEE-EW! Is that you, Bertie?

You stink, smelly pants," sniffed Suzy.

I'm not the only one who stinks,
thought Bertie.

When Mom farts, she coughs at the same time to cover it up.

When Dad lets off, he's so sneaky...

...you don't know what's coming until it hits you.

Grandma's always letting go.

She just blames the cat.

Suzy claims she never farts.

TOOT
PLAPPER
PIN

But she sounds like a brass band when she thinks no one's listening!

And when the dog farts, he fans it all around!

But Bertie does it best ...

Especially in the bath!

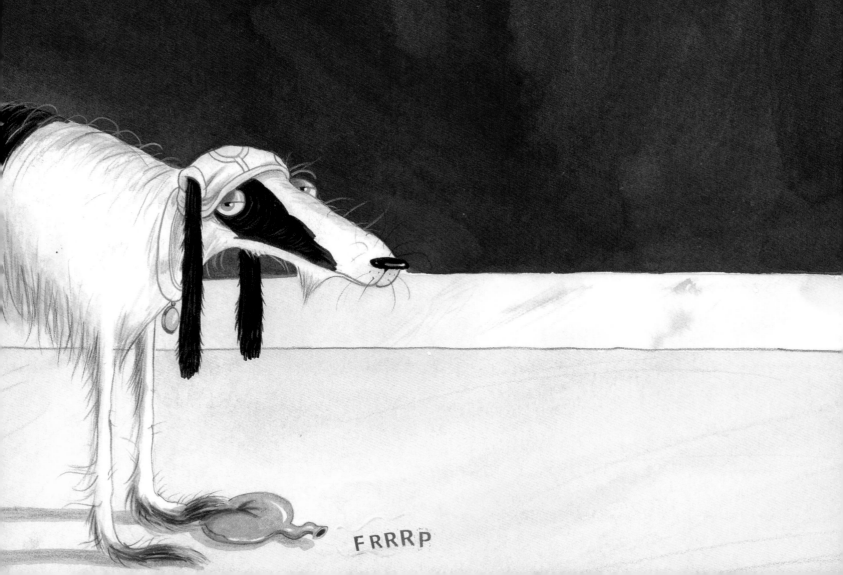

FRRRP